Our Principal Promised to Kiss a Pig

Kalli Dakos and Alicia DesMarteau

Illustrated by Carl DiRocco

Albert Whitman & Company, Morton Grove, Illinois

For the memory of my Aunt Irene,
whose love of great literature
inspired my childhood,
and for the entire Sperdakos Family.—K.D.

To God for saving me,
and to Grandma for making me Greek noodles.—A.D.

For Gina, James, David, and Mark.—C.D.

Library of Congress Cataloging-in-Publication Data

Dakos, Kalli.
Our principal promised to kiss a pig / by Kalli Dakos and Alicia DesMarteau;
illustrated by Carl DiRocco.
p. cm.
Summary: When the school principal promises to kiss a pig if the students read 10,000 books,
a girl volunteers Hamlet, her unwilling, Shakespeare-quoting pet pig.
ISBN 0-8075-6629-2 (hardcover)
[1. Books and reading-Fiction. 2. Pigs-Fiction. 3. School principals-Fiction. 4. Schools-Fiction.
5. Shakespeare, William, 1564-1616-Fiction.]
I. DesMarteau, Alicia. II. DiRocco, Carl, 1963- ill. III. Title.
PZ7.D15223Ou 2004 [Fic]-dc22 2003026210

The design is by Carol Gildar.

For more information about Albert Whitman & Company,
please visit our web site at www.albertwhitman.com.

My pet pig Hamlet knows about broken hearts,
and it's all my fault.

It started in September when the principal of my school said she would kiss a pig if the students read lots of books. Ms. Juliet loves to do crazy things to get us to read. Last year she went up in a hot air balloon, even though she is terrified of heights, and her screams were so loud they scared the toupee off the gym teacher's head.

Another year she sat on the roof of the school for an entire day and read books. When it started to rain, she put on scuba-diving goggles and a snorkel and kept right on reading.

This year she has promised to kiss a pig if we read 10,000 books.

It just so happened that I had a pig! My aunt won a pet pig at the state fair last year and gave him to me when she moved into an apartment that doesn't allow pets. She teaches high school students about a man called William Shakespeare. He was a writer hundreds of years ago. People spoke a funny kind of English back then, and had weird names like Romeo, Touchstone, and Hamlet. My aunt thought it would be funny to name her pig Hamlet.

Without even thinking, I told Ms. Juliet all about my pig and volunteered him for the kiss. Poor Hamlet! When I told him, he looked as if I was going to make him eat a ham sandwich.

I should never have opened my big mouth and said Ms. Juliet could kiss him in front of the entire school. I wouldn't want someone to kiss **me** in front of hundreds of people. Why would a pig feel any differently?

All the kids at school started reading. By the end of November, we had read 1,428 books. Ms. Juliet made us figure out how many more we had to read.

$$10,000 - 1,428 = 8,572 \ books$$

At least Hamlet didn't have to kiss the principal . . . yet.

But I knew he was worried when I found him at the stove stirring pizza sauce, mud, and prune juice in a huge pot. I think he was trying to make a magic potion to stop the kiss!

PRUNE JUICE

Pizza Sauce

By the end of April, we had read 4,702 books. We still had 5,298 left. The school year was nearly over, and we hadn't even read half the books to win the contest!

In May, two things happened. An author came to visit our school, and we had the best book fair in the world.

One girl in my class bought 26 books with her dog-walking money and read every single one of them. A lot of kids started reading the author's books, and before long we had read 8,987 books.

Hamlet was miserable. I guess his potion didn't work.

The third week in May, Hamlet's fate
was sealed. The kids had read 10,682 books and were
still reading.

A day in June was picked for the kiss. The
newspaper planned to send a reporter and a
photographer. The gym was decorated with over
10,000 hearts and lips—one for every book we'd read.
The night before the big kiss, Hamlet stayed in my
room. Neither of us could sleep.

The next morning, I put Hamlet in the baby's car seat, and my mother drove us to school. I felt sick inside, and didn't even want to imagine how Hamlet felt.

But when we arrived at school, I saw a stubborn look on Hamlet's face.

All the world's a stage,
And one pig in his time
Plays many parts.

I must be a soldier
In this kissing war—
The battle starts!

WE WANT THE KISS!!

The kids cheered when I walked into the gym with Hamlet. We walked past 10,983 hearts and lips to a big table. I put Hamlet on the table and stayed beside him for support. What was going to happen next?

Ms. Juliet walked into the gym and the students cheered again. When Hamlet saw her, he gasped and nearly fell off the table. Then his eyes lit up as if the sun, the moon, and the stars had all *come out* at once. I could tell he had changed his mind about kissing Ms. Juliet!

Ms. Juliet announced, "Congratulations, students. You have won the contest again this year. Now I will honor my promise and kiss this . . . pig." She leaned over to kiss Hamlet on the snout. Hamlet leaned forward, too, ready and waiting for the kiss . . . but it never came.

Then in the silence of the gym, Ms. Juliet took a step away from Hamlet and said in a voice that was just above a whisper, "I was able to sit on the roof of the school for an entire day, even in the rain. I was able to go up in that hot air balloon, even though I am afraid of heights. But the very thought of kissing a pig brings dirt, mud, and slop to my mind, and I can't do it. I just can't!"

The kids started yelling, "You have to kiss the pig. You promised! You promised!"

Ms. Juliet looked around the room at the hearts and lips, the photographer, the reporter, the teachers, and the students. Then she looked at Hamlet, who was almost in tears.

Ms. Juliet moved closer to the table where Hamlet was waiting, leaned over, and looked into his eyes. As if in a dream, Hamlet gazed back at her.

Then Ms. Juliet puckered her lips and kissed Hamlet on the snout—not once, not twice, but three times! Hamlet looked as though he was going to faint.

All the kids clapped and cheered. Hamlet was still in a daze when I picked him up. His eyes were round and dopey and glued to Ms. Juliet.

Did my heart love till now?
I never loved till I met thou!

Hamlet wasn't the same
after the big kiss. He couldn't sleep,
he hardly ate, and he moped around
the house.

Ms. Juliet, my star above,
I no sooner looked than loved.

I'll be sad today and tomorrow,
For parting is such sweet sorrow.

I was worried about him, so I was relieved when my aunt told me she'd won another pig at the state fair this year—a girl pig! My aunt named her Kate and brought her over to keep Hamlet company. I think Hamlet's broken heart is healing fast.

Shall I compare thee to a summer's day?
Thou art more lovely in every way.
If this be a dream, I shall not wake.
I long for you to kiss me, Kate!

I send my dearest kiss to you.
Goodnight, sweet pig.
I love you, too!

There's one thing our story proves—
The course of true love **can** run smooth!

Shakespearean References

William Shakespeare was an English playwright, poet, and actor who lived from 1564 to 1616. He worked in the theatrical world of London in the 1500s and 1600s and wrote some of English literature's greatest plays, including **Hamlet, Romeo and Juliet, A Midsummer Night's Dream, As You Like It, Macbeth, Julius Caesar, Othello, King Lear,** and **The Tempest.** Many people believe that Shakespeare is English literature's greatest author, and his works are still performed, read, and loved by people around the world today.

He is also the favorite writer of Hamlet the pig.

p. 9: **To kiss, or not to kiss,**
The principal in school?
Hamlet: act 3, scene 1, line 56
Hamlet: To be, or not to be—that is
the question . . .

p. 11: **Double, double, toil and trouble,**
Let their plans burn and bubble!
Macbeth: act 4, scene 1, lines 10–11
Witches: Double, double toil
and trouble,
Fire burn and cauldron bubble.

p. 13: **Out, out, brief candle**
With so small a light!
Macbeth: act 5, scene 5, line 23.
Macbeth: Out, out, brief candle . . .

p. 15: **O, heavy heart, do not weep.**
This kiss has murdered sleep.
Macbeth: act 2, scene 2, line 39
Macbeth: ". . . Macbeth does
murder sleep"—

p. 16: **O, horrible! O, horrible!**
Most horrible!
Hamlet: act 1, scene 5, line 80
Ghost of Hamlet's father: O, horrible!
O, horrible! Most horrible!

p. 17: **All the world's a stage,**
And one pig in his time
Plays many parts.
As You Like It: act 2, scene 7,
lines 138–41
Jacques: All the world's a stage, . . .
And one man in his time plays
many parts . . .

p. 19: **A pig to himself must be true,**
In spite of plans that humans
brew.
Hamlet: act 1, scene 3, line 77
Polonius: This above all, to thine own
self be true . . .

p. 21: **I never saw true beauty**
Till this day.
Romeo and Juliet: act 1, scene 5, line 54
Romeo: For I ne'er saw true beauty
till this night.

p. 21: **Ms. Juliet is the sun**
That lights my way!
Romeo and Juliet: act 2, scene 2,
lines 2–3
Romeo: But soft! What light through
yonder window breaks?
It is the east, and Juliet is the sun!

p. 21: Whoever loved
That loved not at first sight?
As You Like It: act 3, scene 5, line 82
Phebe: "Who ever loved that loved
not at first sight?"
(Here Shakespeare quotes the
playwright Christopher Marlowe.)

p. 25: What's in a name like pig
or boar?
*Romeo and Juliet: act 2, scene 2,
lines 43-44*
Juliet: What's in a name? That which
we call a rose
By any other word would smell
as sweet.

p. 27: Did my heart love till now?
*Romeo and Juliet: act 1, scene 5,
line 53*
Romeo: Did my heart love till now?

p. 28: I no sooner looked than loved.
*As You Like It: act 5, scene 2,
lines 31-32*
Rosalind: . . . for your brother and
my sister . . . no sooner looked but
they loved . . .

p. 28: I'll be sad today and tomorrow,
For parting is such sweet sorrow.
*Romeo and Juliet: act 2, scene 2,
lines 185-86*
Juliet: Parting is such sweet sorrow
That I shall say good night till it
be morrow.

p. 29: Shall I compare thee to a
summer's day?
Thou art more lovely in every way.
Shakespeare's sonnet 18:
Shall I compare thee to a
summer's day?
Thou art more lovely and
more temperate.

p. 29: If this be a dream, I shall not wake.
I long for you to kiss me, Kate!
*The Taming of the Shrew: act 5,
scene 2, line 186*
Petruchio: Come on and kiss
me, Kate!

p. 29: Goodnight, sweet pig.
Hamlet: act 5, scene 2, line 342
Horatio: Good night, sweet prince . . .

p. 30: There's one thing our story
proves—
The course of true love can
run smooth!
*A Midsummer Night's Dream: act 1,
scene 1, line 134*
Lysander: The course of true love
never did run smooth . . .

**Back
cover:** Friends, teachers, students,
Lend me your ears.
Julius Caesar: act 3, scene 2, line 73
Antony: Friends, Romans,
countrymen, lend me your ears.

*All quotations and line numbers are from Orgel, Stephen, and A. R. Braunmuller, eds. **The Complete Pelican Shakespeare.** New York: Penguin Putnam, Inc., 2002.*